RACE THE WILD
RAIN FOREST RELAY

RACE THE WILD

ARE YOU READY TO RUN THE WILDEST RACE OF YOUR LIFE?

Course #1: Rain Forest Relay

Course #2: Great Reef Games

RACE THE WILD

RAIN FOREST RELAY

·BY **KRISTIN EARHART**·
·ILLUSTRATED BY **EDA KABAN**·

SCHOLASTIC INC.

TO JENNE, WHO KNOWS WHAT IT MEANS TO BE ON A TEAM —KJE

Text copyright © 2015 by Kristin Earhart.
Illustrations copyright © 2015 by Scholastic Inc.

ISBN 978-0-545-77353-9

12 11 10 9 8 7 6 5 4 3 2   15 16 17 18 19 20/0

Printed in the U.S.A.   40
First printing 2015

Book design by Yaffa Jaskoll

CONGRATULATIONS!

Your team has been chosen to compete in **THE WILD LIFE**, a race around the world to experience the majesty of the animal kingdom.

Be the first team to answer all the clues and you'll win the ultimate prize—a million dollars for the team.

There are four legs, each in a different habitat. At every stop, you'll meet strange and wonderful animals. Keep your eyes and ears open for clues. And watch out—the wild world is beautiful, but it can also be dangerous!

GOOD LUCK!

CHAPTER 1

SEEING RED

Russell Dean watched as the other contestants came into the clearing. They had all said good-bye to their parents the day before and boarded a plane. Russell had barely ever left his home-town. Now he was far away, in the middle of nowhere. Well, not exactly nowhere. It was the most awesome place he had ever seen.

The trees rose over one hundred feet, and their thick leaves blocked out almost all the sun-light. The warm, moist air clung to his skin, giving him the chills. Everything on the forest floor was cloaked in spooky green shadows. When he looked up, it was like a kaleidoscope of green with slivers of golden light. This place felt special, almost sacred.

When Russell looked down again, the clearing was full of people: mostly kids around his age and a few adults with clipboards. Russell hadn't paid much attention to the other kids the day before, because he'd been with his best friends: Jayden, Dallas, Damien, and Gabe. They'd played flag football together for three years. Even though they'd all wanted to be contestants on *The Wild Life*, it had been Russell's idea to enter.

But now he didn't have a choice. He had to deal with the other kids. He wasn't with his friends anymore.

"Welcome," a man called out. "I am Bull Gordon." The man was standing behind a podium, but not the kind of podium that a principal stands behind at an assembly. This one was made from the trunk of an old tree, with roots reaching into the ground like spindly fingers. The man stretched his arms and wrapped them around the top of the podium's crusty bark.

"You are in the heart of the Amazon rain forest, home to some of the world's most exotic animals," he bellowed. "For all you lucky contestants, this is the start of the Wild Life competition—the first of four legs, each in a different ecosystem. To win, you'll have to prove that you understand what makes these different environments work." Bull paused and surveyed the contestants. "Now, you need to find your teams. And hurry up! This is a race after all." A sly smile gave way to the trademark grin that showed up on all the ads for *The Wild Life*.

"Hey, you!" Russell heard a voice call. The voice seemed to be directed at him. "You, with the red folder." The voice sounded impatient.

Russell looked down at the folder in his hand. It was definitely red, unlike the ones his four friends had. Theirs were all green.

"What? Are you going to make us come to you? Fine." In no time, the voice and its owner were in Russell's face. "What's your deal?" The voice belonged to a girl. The girl was tall, and she had a red folder tucked under one arm. A hiking backpack dangled from the other. "You're on our team. I'm Sage Stevens." Sage turned around and pointed to a much shorter girl whose long dark hair was pulled into a braid so thick that it looked like a panther's tail. "This is Mari Soto."

Next, Sage pointed at a boy. The boy had a gigantic camera hanging around his neck. It was almost bigger than his head.

"And this is—"

"Dev Patel, at your service," the boy said, cutting Sage off. He politely stretched out his hand.

Russell gave it a shake.

"And you are?" Sage Stevens prompted. Her intense blue eyes returned their gaze to Russell. She tucked her shoulder-length hair behind her ear.

"I'm Russell," he answered. "Russell Dean."

"And what would you say your strengths will be?" Sage asked, eyebrows raised. "In the race, I mean. What do you have to offer the team?"

Russell wasn't about to answer. Who put this girl in change? She was getting on his nerves.

"There's a million dollars up for grabs," Sage said, as if Russell didn't already know that. "As a team, we need to be fast, generous, and smart if we are going to win *The Wild Life*."

Russell knew all about the race. He didn't need Sage's advice. After all, it had been his idea to enter in the first place. He was the one who had sent his friends the link. It was a once-in-a-lifetime chance to travel to the world's most exotic places and see wildlife up close. Plus, there were challenges that meant real adventure: mountain climbing, river rafting, maybe even a safari. That's why it was called *The Wild Life*!

Russell couldn't believe that his friends were all on a team together, and he had ended up with a bunch of strangers. He'd even been the one to talk Damien's mom into letting him go. Russell had promised he'd look out for him.

He glanced over and saw Damien and his other friends, laughing together. They hadn't said a word to him since they found out he had been booted from their team. They hadn't been mean, but they hadn't been particularly nice about it either. "Who knew they'd change the number on a team from five to four?" Gabe had said, like it was a random piece of trivia. The worst part was that Russell knew his friends. He knew they were smart and fast. He knew that they had come here to win.

"And tough," Russell said after a long pause. He looked at each of his new team members in turn.

"What?" Sage asked.

"Fast, generous, smart, and tough," stated Russell. "We'll also need to be tough if we want to be the winning team."

Sage nodded, and the corners of her mouth turned down. Russell could tell she was holding back a smile. Dev and Mari nodded, too.

"Now, groups," Bull announced over the

excited frenzy, "you have two duties. First, get to know your teammates. Second, get some sleep. Tomorrow, when the sun rises, you will receive your first challenge. Have a good night." He stepped away from the podium and began talking to one of the adults with a clipboard.

Russell leaned over, grabbed his bag, and swung it over his back. He turned to Sage, Mari, and Dev. "Anyone know the way to the red team's bunk?" he asked.

THE AMAZON RAIN FOREST

A rain forest is just what you would guess: a forest with extremely high amounts of rainfall, usually between 80 and 250 inches a year. It is very humid, which means there is a lot of moisture in the air. The temperature is warm all year. It usually ranges from 68 to 93 degrees Fahrenheit (20 to 34 degrees Celsius).

Rain forests cover only 2% of the earth, but they are home to over 50% of the world's species. That means over half of the different kinds of animals in the world live in rain forests.

The Amazon, in South America, is the largest rain forest in the world. The heart of the rain forest is the Amazon River, which runs over 4,000 miles, from the Andes Mountains to the Atlantic Ocean.

GUYANA
SURINAME
FRENCH GUIANA
VENEZUELA
COLOMBIA
ECUADOR
River
Amazon
AMAZON
RAIN FOREST
PERU
BRAZIL
BOLIVIA
PARAGUAY
CHILE
ARGENTINA
URUGUAY
PACIFIC OCEAN
ATLANTIC OCEAN

CHAPTER 2

CALLING ALL CUCKOOS

"**M**y dad laughed when he read the rules," Sage said, putting a scarlet hoodie in her backpack. "He says it's hilarious that we can't use cell phones or computers."

"Adults assume we can't do anything without the Internet," Mari added. There was a snap as she finished twisting a rubber band around her braid.

"I can't believe I have to leave my camera behind," Dev said with a sigh. "Even worse, I had to trade it for an 'ancam.' That isn't even a cool name. What is it, a combination of an animal and a camera?" He was comparing his ultra-advanced camera to the tiny device that all the contestants had received that afternoon. "This thing doesn't even have a decent telephoto lens. We're going to have to get super close to get our shots."

The ancam was a digital camera and walkie-talkie combo made just for the race. All the race devices were set up to call only one number: the Wild Life hotline. Teams could use it to contact the race organizers to get new clues . . . or if they got into trouble. The organizers used the devices to send maps or other information to the contestants.

"At least the ancam is fair," Mari said. "All the teams have the same stuff."

"And cell phones wouldn't get a signal in the Amazon anyway," Russell reminded them.

"If they did," Dev chimed in, "I bet the green team would be calling their mommies every five minutes."

Everyone laughed, even Russell. He could tell that Dev had just picked a team at random to make fun of. Dev wasn't trying to be mean, just funny. Russell hadn't told his new teammates that he was friends with everyone on the green team. Now definitely did not seem like the right time. The funny thing about Dev's joke was that Dallas's mom had this awesome tech job. Her company made cutting-edge phones and other smart devices. Dallas's house was full of cool stuff. If anyone would have a way of contacting his mom from the Amazon, it was Dallas.

The four members of the red team were in the middle of packing their bags. *The Wild Life* started the next day. They'd carry only a backpack during the race. The organizers would take the rest of their stuff to the next stop so it would be waiting for them.

Marcia and Javier headed up the Wild Life clothing and supply crew, and they were in the red team's bunkhouse, advising the team on their wardrobe and gear.

"You all need to take a red backpack and a red rain poncho," Marcia said, "but picking the rest is up to you. You get twenty pieces in all."

Each team member could choose from a whole rack of athletic clothes and shoes. Since they were the red team, everything was in some shade of red.

"Is it good or bad that we're red?" Russell

asked. "We won't be camouflaged. Other teams will totally be able to spot us."

"I'm more worried about getting lost," Mari replied. "If we get lost, really lost, a bright red poncho won't help at all. What do we do then?"

"Don't get lost," Sage said in a matter-of-fact tone. "We have to stick together."

"That's good advice," Javier said with a laugh.

But Mari, Dev, and Russell all glanced at one another. It wasn't as if they were going to get lost on purpose.

"If you do lose track of the team, you could use one of these," Javier offered, holding up something that looked like a kazoo. He put it to his lips, and out came a sound that seemed to be half laugh and half squawk. Javier blew again, and the odd, musical chuckle repeated.

"Oh, is that the call of a squirrel cuckoo bird?" Mari asked.

Javier blinked several times and then stared at Mari. He looked down at the wooden instrument. "*Piaya cayana*," he read out loud.

"Oh, yeah," Mari said. "I think that's the scientific name for squirrel cuckoo."

Javier turned the instrument in his hand. He rubbed his finger over a carving on the other side. "What do you know? Squirrel cuckoo," he read.

"What?" Dev questioned. "I thought the squirrel and the cuckoo bird were two totally different animals. Mari, how'd you know that?"

"I don't know," Mari responded. "I probably saw it on TV or something. It has a very distinct call." She didn't look up, but instead investigated a number of tank tops, running her fingertips along the seams.

Russell joined Mari when she moved to the table with the shoe options.

Did he want sports sandals that could get wet? Hiking boots for protection? Or running shoes for speed?

"What shoes are you guys getting?" he asked.

"You need two pairs," Sage said. " 'Cause they'll get wet, and there's nothing worse than wet feet."

Russell sighed. Sage had no problem giving advice. He reached for a pair of sandals like the ones he had worn last year.

"Don't even think about choosing something

that does not have closed toes," Sage added. "There are roots sticking out of the forest floor, creepy crawlies, piranhas. You get the idea."

Russell quickly angled his hand toward a pair of running shoes and some rubber boots. Next, he checked out the extra gear: ropes, climbing belts, a whittling knife.

The four made their final selections, and Marcia and Javier packed up the remaining clothes and shoes. "Bye, Team Red. See you at the send-off," Marcia said, waving.

"Here you go," said Javier, placing a squirrel cuckoo call in the palm of each kid's hand. "On the house. Good luck, guys."

Dev locked the bunk door and looked at his watch. "Twelve hours," he said. "Twelve hours and our lives will change forever."

Russell glanced at the two photos he had put in the outer pocket of his backpack: one was of him and his big sister with their parents; the other was of Russell with Dallas, Damien, Jayden, and Gabe. Russell didn't have to wait a single hour. Some things about his life had already changed.

Russell's brain still felt blurry, despite the fact that Sage had blown the squirrel cuckoo whistle over an hour earlier. Russell didn't need an hour to get ready. He needed more sleep. If Sage didn't chill out, she would drive him cuckoo.

The jungle was alive with chirps and squawks, but the contestants were all silent. The morning mist lingered in the tops of the trees, sheltering the forest floor from the sun.

Russell glanced at his teammates. He hoped they were ready.

"Hey, dude." Russell turned toward the hushed voice and saw Dallas standing next to him. His friend had on a pair of deep green cargo shorts and a gray swim shirt with green on the shoulders. "I just wanted to say have a good race. We're all rooting for you."

"Thanks, man," Russell said. He grabbed Dallas's hand like they always did after good football plays. Then they slapped each other on the back. For a moment, Dallas's hand rested on Russell's red pack.

Russell watched Dallas return to the green team. Dallas gave them all a thumbs-up, and Russell's friends looked at him and waved. They

were all smiling, which was weird. They never smiled before a game; they were all business.

"You know those guys?" Dev asked.

"Yeah," Russell admitted. "They're my friends from football."

"How come you're on our team?" Sage wondered.

"Got me. But I am," Russell said. He caught Sage staring at him, studying his face.

"Look. Bull's coming," Mari whispered. The teams instinctively moved into tighter clusters. The yellow team—two girls and two boys—wore matching lemon-colored polo shirts and khaki shorts. Next to the yellow team, the blue team looked like a varsity sports photo. They were all in athletic shorts and tanks, with long, strong arms and legs. The purple and orange teams were gathered closer to the podium. To Russell, the orange team looked more like the red team—a good mix. The purple team was all girls. The green team was all boys. Even as he tried to get a sense of the different teams, Russell realized they had one thing in common. They all wanted to win.

"Morning!" Bull announced from behind his tree podium. "And a very good morning it is!" He paused as a few kids mumbled a response. "Excuse me. You're about to race in *The Wild Life*. Is it a good morning or not?"

"Yes!" the contestants cheered. The sound seemed to stay in the clearing, echoing back on the small crowd.

"Well, you have your gear. You know the rules, so there's no reason not to start. Punch the answer to the first clue into your ancams, and get going." He paused and tipped his fedora forward for effect. The teams waited for his cue. "What's the name of the of the life source that snakes through the rain forest all the way to the Atlantic Ocean? Answer it, and go!"

CREATURE FEATURE

SQUIRREL CUCKOO

SCIENTIFIC NAME: *Piaya cayana*

TYPE: bird

RANGE: from Mexico to Argentina and Uruguay, and on Trinidad

FOOD: large insects, including caterpillars and wasps; sometimes spiders, small lizards, and cocoa beans; rarely fruit

This cuckoo bird gets its name from its habit of running along tree limbs. It likes to jump from branch to branch, much like a squirrel. It doesn't fly very often. The squirrel cuckoo nests high in the trees.

CHAPTER 3

THE BiGGEST SNAKE

Easy! If he couldn't answer this question, he didn't deserve to be here. "Here," Russell prompted, snatching the ancam from Dev. He fumbled with the new device and got to the alphabet screen. A-M-A-Z-O-N_R-I-V-E-R, he typed with super-speed thumbs. He'd have to tell his mom that all those video games were good for something after all. The screen lit up with a picture of leaves that spelled *CORRECT*. Next, the screen read *YOUR NEXT CLUE*.

"I got it! I got it!" Russell called in a hushed

voice. He could see kids from other teams glance over at him. Sage, Mari, and Dev pulled in tight to look at his screen.

```
What has feet like a duck, the
body of a beaver, and the head of
a hairy hippo?
```

```
Warning: At least half the animal
has to be out of the water in
your photo.
```

What? This one was not easy. Russell realized the first question about the Amazon had been a freebie. Now the race had really begun.

"I know it," Mari said quietly. "Let's get down to the closest stream."

"What is it?" Sage demanded, but Mari had already headed down a narrow path at a steady jog.

Russell handed the ancam back to Dev. Then he fell in line after Mari and Sage, thinking they were one step ahead of the rest of the teams. But soon the other kids started darting past them. Russell noticed blue jerseys veering from the path to pass other teams. Why was Mari moving so slowly?

"Can we move faster?" he urged, wanting to be first to the stream. They had already lost the lead he had earned them with his fast finger work on the ancam.

"Mari?" Sage prompted.

"Steady," the other girl replied, her long braid swaying gracefully with her even pace.

From up ahead came the sound of eager splashes in the water, then the thrust of canoes sliding into the stream. Russell glanced at Dev and rolled his eyes. If Mari knew the answer to the clue, why was she holding them back? Russell was starting to wonder if she knew it after all.

When the red team came to the muddy bank, the other teams were already thirty feet downstream, laughing and yelling at one another. Russell could see Damien slap his paddle on the murky water.

Mari sat down on a smooth rock and eased off her running shoes.

"What are you doing?" Russell demanded.

"Shhhh. I'm putting on my rubber boots," said Mari. "Sage is right, there's nothing worse than soggy feet."

"But they're getting way ahead," Russell pointed out. Dev did not say anything, but he stood next to Russell, his hands on his hips. Sage busied herself readying a canoe.

Mari slipped on one boot. "They're also scaring away all the wildlife. They'll never get a picture of a capybara if there aren't any capybaras to be found." Mari pulled on the other boot, stood up, and grabbed a paddle.

The capybara! Russell had read about it, but he never would have figured out the clue that quickly.

"We can go now," Mari said, "and maybe we should consider heading upstream, away from the other teams. We can approach more quietly."

"Yeah," Dev said, endorsing Mari's tactic. "Then we have a better shot at getting our . . . shot."

Russell allowed himself a second to smile at Dev's joke.

When they moved toward the canoes, they realized Javier, whom they had met the day before, was there, leaning against a paddle. "So we meet again, Team Red. I'll be your chaperone."

Russell was happy to see Javier. In *The Wild Life*, all the teams had a guide, but the guide was only there for safety—and to reinforce the rules of the game. The contestants could not rely on the guide for hints or directions. Still, it helped to have someone cool tagging along, and Russell definitely thought Javier was cool.

Then they were off, the bows of the boats gliding through the murky green water. Sage had taken the front end of the canoe that Javier had climbed into. Mari was the middle. That had left the other canoe for Dev and Russell. Russell sat in the back, because he thought he'd be stronger at paddling. Dev was tall, but lanky.

The team was silent for a long time. Trees and plants grew to the very edges of the banks. Everything was oversized: palm fronds as big as kayaks, lily pads the size of kiddie pools.

It seemed quiet, but Russell knew that there was life at every level of the trees and in the stream. "Do you think there are piranhas under our boat?" he wondered out loud.

"Probably," Sage answered quickly. Then everyone went quiet again.

"We must be close," Mari announced. "There are footprints in the mud." Russell followed her gaze. "They are such unusual rodents. They have webbed feet." Mari smiled and shook her head.

When they went around a bend, Dev leaned forward. "Whoa, is that it?" he whispered rather loudly. They all looked to where he pointed. There stood an animal the size of a large pig. Its reddish-brown hair looked like brush bristles, and its nose was dark and wide. "It's huge."

"It is the largest rodent in the world," Mari said.

Russell noticed something moving on the ground behind it. A snake! "Quick! Get the shot before that snake scares it into the water!"

Just as Dev pulled out his ancam, Russell heard a loud splash behind them.

"Hey, that must be it!" Damien yelled as a Team Green canoe sliced through the water and knocked the side of Dev and Russell's boat.

"I got it!" cried Gabe from the green team's other canoe. He shook his ancam in the air.

Russell's gaze lingered on Dev, who had fallen to the floor of the canoe. Just as Russell glanced back to the side of the stream, the capybara slipped under the water's surface. He gritted his teeth.

"Nice!" Dallas called out. The green team was cheering and slapping high fives. "Send it to Bull Gordon. Now." When he said the last word, Dallas looked Russell in the eye. A second later, the four boys and their guide were off down the stream.

"Seriously?" Sage said. "They stole our shot."

"My picture's all blurry," Dev confessed. "I took it right when they slammed into us." His eyes narrowed.

Even though Dallas was his friend, Russell thought it was a slimy move. "Let's just wait here," he said. "The capybara's got to come up sooner or later."

"They can hold their breath for five minutes," Mari said.

They had been waiting for a minute or two when they saw something move on the nearby bank again.

"It's just the snake," Dev said.

"That's not just any snake," Mari noted. "It's an anaconda. The largest snake in the world. An anconda can eat something up to half its weight. It'd eat a capybara. They aren't picky."

But the anaconda was not headed in the direction of the giant rodent, it was swimming toward the canoes.

"That guy is big," he said. "If it can eat something half its weight, it would probably eat . . ."

". . . us," Sage finished.

CREATURE FEATURE

CAPYBARA

SCIENTIFIC NAME: *Hydrochoerus hydrochaeris*

TYPE: mammal

RANGE: Brazil, Columbia, Uruguay, Venezuela, and parts of Argentina

FOOD: mostly grass and water plants; occasionally fruit, grains, and bark

The capybara's body is made for its semi-aquatic lifestyle. It spends half its time in the water! Its webbed feet are like small flippers, making the rodent a better swimmer. But the capybara also has distinct toes (four on each front foot, three on the back). The toes help it move around well on land, too.

Because its eyes, ears, and nose are near the top of its head, the capybara can breathe, see, and smell while it is floating, nearly hidden, in the water—just like a hippo!

CHAPTER 4
CLEAR AS GLASS

Everyone went silent. Russell didn't even blink. Having his best friends swoop in and steal the red team's shot was bad enough, but getting squeezed to death by an anaconda would be so much worse.

Russell looked down. He could see the green-and-black pattern just below the water's surface. The snake's body was as thick as his thigh. He tried not to think of the pictures he had seen of an anaconda after a meal—a huge lump in the middle of its body, an entire dinner eaten in a single gulp. Russell's head felt fuzzy. He held his breath, careful not to move.

"When an anaconda attacks," Mari whispered, "it wraps around its prey. Each time the victim exhales, the anaconda tightens its hold."

Russell looked at Mari in disbelief. How could she talk about that at a time like this? Russell could feel the boat gently rocking as the scaly snake wriggled by. Its long, winding body sent ripples through the stream.

"Sounds breathtaking," Dev said. This time, Russell didn't smile at his teammate's joke. Didn't Dev realize how dangerous an anaconda could be?

Once the snake was far enough away, Russell released a big sigh.

"Don't worry. No one will suffocate on my watch," Javier said, but Russell had seen Javier's face when the snake swam under their canoes.

"Hey, guys," Sage said in a soft voice. "Over there."

When Russell squinted in the morning sun, he could see several sets of eyes, nostrils, and rounded ears poking out of the water.

"Oh, it's a whole group of capybaras," Mari said. "That makes sense. They hardly ever live alone."

Dev targeted his ancam immediately. "I'm not going to miss my shot again," he murmured. As if on cue, a young capybara stumbled onto the bank. The ancam went *click, click, click*. "Got it!" Dev yelled before the rodent disappeared into the water again.

"Send it to Bull Gordon," Sage said at once.

Dev clicked a few buttons, and the group heard the motor of the tiny camera/walkie-talkie rev. In just a few seconds, Dev read out loud the message he had received. "It's a clue," he said.

Whose heart beats from
inside glass?

He frowned and looked at his teammates.

Russell did the same. *A heart inside glass?* That sounded like some bizarre medical operation, not something you would find in the rain forest.

"I think I know this one, too," Mari said, almost too quiet to hear.

"Really?" Russell asked. Everyone turned and

looked at Mari, who was absentmindedly strok-
ing her braid.

"Yeah," Mari said. She slowly tilted her head
from side to side, like she was tossing ideas
around in her brain. "I mean, it's a tricky clue, but
there is the glass frog. It lives in the rain forest."

"A glass frog?" Dev questioned.

Mari shook her head. "Not real glass. It just
has nearly clear skin on his stomach, so you can
actually see its heart and other organs."

"That's it," Sage announced. "I'm sure. So
where will we find one?"

"Near a stream or the river," Mari responded.

"Okay then, let's keep an eye out as we go
downstream," Sage declared. "I don't like that the
green team is so far ahead."

Russell eyed Sage. Why was she giving out orders? Mari was the one who knew all the answers. Even so, Russell agreed that they had to catch up with the other teams.

The rhythm of the paddles sloshing into the water fell in time with the chirps and calls that filled the air. The rain forest was full of life, with trees hundreds of years old and more kinds of plants than anywhere else on Earth. The Amazon River was the heart of the jungle. Thousands of waterways joined it along its path across South America. During the rainy season, many streams overflowed, filling the forest floor with over twenty feet of water.

But it was not the rainy season now. It was drier, which meant the streams were not as full.

Large rocks jutted out of the water, and the red team had to work to paddle around them.

"Hit one of those rocks wrong, and all five of us will have to cram into one canoe," Javier said. Their guide's tone was friendly, but Russell knew it was a real warning.

As they made their way downstream, Russell kept his eyes on the shores.

"If I remember correctly, there are hundreds of species of glass frogs." Mari had to raise her voice over the rush of the water. "But almost all of them have pale green backs."

"Pale green in a rain forest?" Russell repeated. "How are we supposed to see them?"

"We aren't," Mari responded matter-of-factly. "Scientists think the frogs' skin might be camouflage."

How did Mari know all this stuff?

"Look out ahead!" Javier called out.

Russell looked and realized that their stream was about to join another larger, faster stream.

"There are rapids on the left!" Sage yelled. "Stay to the right!"

Russell plunged his paddle deep into the water to make the turn. "Other side!" he belted at Dev as their canoe tilted into the crashing water. Dev yanked his paddle out and quickly dipped it back into the water on the other side, but the water was moving too fast. It ripped the paddle from his hands. Now Russell had to steer alone, and there were more rapids up ahead.

"Sorry," Dev yelled over the water.

With Javier at the stern, the other canoe swept

smoothly down the stream, avoiding the jagged rocks.

Dev grasped both sides of the canoe, trying to keep it upright by sheer will. "Wait!" he called out. "Look over there!"

"I'm not exactly in the position for sightseeing," Russell reminded his teammate between his quick, short breaths. But a glance over his shoulder was all it took. Behind him, on the far shore, he saw the green team cheering. There was a stream of rapids and rocks between them.

They all assumed the same thing: The green team had found the answer to clue number three.

"Let's get to the other bank," Sage yelled back to Dev and Russell. "We can backtrack on land."

Russell wrenched his paddle from side to side, trying to redirect the canoe. Even though he didn't have a paddle, Dev shifted his weight to help move the boat in the right direction. They were both out of breath by the time they rammed their canoe into the tall grass.

"I'll stay with the canoes," Javier said. "And keep an eye out."

Russell nodded. He didn't want to say what he was thinking, that it was a good idea. He wouldn't put it past the green team to push their canoes into the water—and strand the red team on shore.

They clambered out of the canoes and began to hike upstream. "Start looking now," Sage said.

The plant growth was thicker close to the river where more sun snuck through to the forest floor. They pushed through branches and vines, skirting ferns on the ground. Even though his legs were wet with sweat, Russell was glad to have on long cargo pants for protection.

"I think I found one," Dev called. "Let me see if it has a clear belly." The others turned to look just as he reached toward a tiny frog with a vivid green-and-black pattern.

"No!" Mari screeched. "It's poisonous!"

Dev jerked his hand back, still staring at the little frog sitting innocently on a log.

"It's a poison dart frog," Mari declared. "That pattern is supposed to be a warning. You could get really sick touching that."

"It's green," Dev said, stunned.

"They come in blue, yellow, red, and green. And they're all toxic. Some can kill you. The frog we want won't have bold markings," Mari said, and they all headed off again. Dev held his hand in a nervous fist.

It wasn't long before they reached a small clearing. Several trees grew along the river's edge. "Where should we look?" Sage asked, her question directed at Mari.

"Probably under a clump of leaves," Mari said, "where they can stay wet."

Russell had to wonder what they would do without Mari. She seemed to be a wildlife genius.

"Found one!" Mari announced almost immediately. She plucked a pale green frog off a skinny branch and held it in the air. All four kids looked up and gazed right through the clear skin at the inner workings of the frog.

"Is that its heart beating?" Russell asked.

"Yep," affirmed Mari, as Dev took a shot with his ancam. "Cool, huh?"

"If you say so," Russell said. "But my first thought was *gross*."

"Did you send the photo in?" Sage asked Dev.

Dev didn't need to answer. He held up the ancam so everyone could read the message from Bull Gordon:

```
Nice work! Next move:
Head to the high ropes.
```

CREATURE FEATURE

POISON DART FROG, ALSO CALLED POISON ARROW FROG

SCIENTIFIC NAME: multiple species, family Dendrobatidae

TYPE: amphibian

RANGE: Central and South America

FOOD: insects

These frogs are toxic. The rain forest's native people use their poison on darts and arrows for hunting.

There are hundreds of species, coming in a range of colors. All are bright or have striking markings that tell other animals, "Steer clear! I've got venom on my skin!" Most live on the forest floor, but some make their home in trees. They live close to water to keep their skin moist.

CHAPTER 5

THE CRAZY CANOPY

It wasn't long before Russell looked up from the canoe to see a dock where several large motorboats were tied. Javier helped pull the canoes ashore and quickly introduced himself to one of the boat captains, who'd take the team to the high-ropes course.

"Hello." The captain tipped his old baseball cap at the teammates. When he grinned, deep wrinkles etched their way across his cocoa-colored skin.

Russell nodded to the captain, and sat down next to Dev. Mari held on to the edge of the boat, easing her way in.

Sage stood behind her. She faced Javier, the captain, and her teammates. "Let's remember, this isn't a sightseeing tour," Sage announced. "It's a race. Speed is a good thing." Then she sat down on the front plank by herself.

Russell wasn't sure what Sage was getting at. Anyone who had actually read the Wild Life packet knew that it paid to be observant. Sometimes there were extra challenges at the end of the race course, and paying attention could really help a team. Winning this race wasn't always about being first.

Soon, the captain began to steer the boat toward a wooden jetty that reached into the river.

"Thanks," Javier told the captain before turning to the kids. "You guys go ahead. I'll meet you here after you get the next clue."

The teammates murmured their good-byes and rushed off the boat and down the jetty. There were lots of signs that read: THE COURSE IN THE CANOPY.

Even without Mari's help, Russell knew what that meant. He'd read about it in school. The canopy was the name for one of the levels of the rain forest.

The top one was the emergent level. It was at the very tips of the trees, where harpy eagles could survey the forest—the treetops looking like fluffy green clouds. The canopy level was just below that, where the thick, leafy branches provided homes and food for all kinds of animals.

The next level down was the understory, which was mostly tree trunks and vines. A few animals lived in the understory, but it was much darker and there wasn't as much food. The bottom level was the forest floor, which was always covered in shadows by the trees above. Prime predators, like the jaguar and ocelot, lived here. For most animals, it was safer taking cover higher up in the trees.

And that's where the red team was headed—into the trees. They quickly found the starting point to the course. There, the workers, wearing matching Course-in-the-Canopy shirts, handed them equipment.

"How do we know these will hold us?" Mari asked as they all stepped into woven nylon harnesses. Russell noticed her hands shaking.

"The harnesses are strong," answered Sage. "And carabiners—these steel loops—can hold hundreds of pounds. We just have to make sure they are locked when we attach them to the ropes."

Mari glanced up warily. Nearly one hundred feet above them, steel ropes stretched from tree to tree like telephone wires.

"Don't worry," Sage said, her voice surprisingly warm. "We'll double-check for you. We'll look out for each other."

Sage was first to climb the ladder. It led to a wooden platform that was built around a thick tree. From there, they would complete several obstacles. Dev followed Sage, then Mari. Russell would be last.

Russell got antsy waiting for Mari. He didn't want to use the word *slow*, but he couldn't believe how precise she was. She grasped each rung of the ladder so carefully it felt like he was waiting forever.

But once they were up top, Mari seemed more at ease. She got across the cargo net without a problem. And the tight rope. Now it was actually Russell who started lagging behind.

Even though he knew it was a race, he slowed down to take it all in. For one thing, he could see a sloth only ten feet away. It was just hanging there, upside down, with yellow claws that looked like they were straight out of a horror film.

As he crossed a huge expanse between trees on a wobbly plank bridge, he stopped and stared

at the world around him. It was entirely different up in the trees. The lush beauty shimmered in the sunlight. The sun blistered down from above with an intense heat.

Now he understood the name. Like a canopy over an old-fashioned bed, the rain forest canopy covered most everything below. It shielded the lower forest from the sun and rain—only small amounts leaked through. Russell saw macaws, cleaning their scarlet feathers with curved beaks; a troop of spider monkeys, plucking fruit from the branches; and lizards, using camouflage to blend into their surroundings. They all called the canopy home.

Over the crunches, squawks, and chatter, Russell could hear the familiar voices of his friends on the green team. They sounded far away, as if they were nearing the end of the course.

"Russell, hurry up," Sage called from the next platform. For once she sounded more encouraging, less insistent. "You've got to see this."

The slim bridge swayed as Russell made his way to the other side.

"Check it out," said Dev.

Russell leaned forward and focused where the others were looking, at a plant that seemed to be growing on one of the branches of a tree. It had lots of tall, spiky leaves and, in its center, there was a tiny pool of water. And there was something in the water.

"Is that—"

"It's a bromeliad," Mari said. "It's in the pineapple family, and it's amazing. It gets its food and water from the air. And it stores its own water, too."

"But what's in the water?" Russell asked.

"They are tadpoles—they'll grow to be poison dart frogs, like the one Dev found earlier. The frogs use the bromeliad as a nursery for their tadpoles. The tadpoles are safer up here than in a stream below."

"But how did it get there?"

"One of the parents carries the tadpoles on its back," Mari said with a shrug.

Russell took a deep breath. It was awesome. There was a tadpole living in a plant, that was living on a giant tree, a hundred feet above ground. Crazy!

"Hey, Russell!" This time it was Dev. "Let's go."

Russell rushed across the stirrup obstacle. It

was like a string of six swings, all dangling from the same wire. It wasn't long before he had caught up. When he did, he realized that they were at the end. The only obstacle left was a zip line that would take them all the way from the treetops to the ground.

Mari stared down, her front teeth digging into her bottom lip.

"It's not that bad," Dev told her. "It's all based on gravity, and you're light, so you won't accelerate as much. Probably sixty miles per hour tops."

Mari's teeth dug deeper.

Sage turned to Russell. "You should go first," she said with her usual authority. He nodded. If Sage, suddenly filled with goodwill, wanted to stay behind and coax Mari onto the zip line, he would let her. But he didn't want to abandon

Mari altogether. He walked up to his team-mate, who was fiddling with her braid. "You'll be fine," he said, but he knew he didn't sound that comforting.

And that's what Russell was thinking about as he whizzed down the zip line at breakneck speed, the wind whipping around him. He should have been thinking of swinging like a spider monkey from tree to tree or soaring like a fierce harpy eagle. Instead, he was worrying about his team-mates getting down safely.

That's when he saw something in a clearing. It appeared man-made, but it also seemed like it belonged in the forest—like it had been there for-ever. It looked like the combination of a stone cross and an ancient tree. He stared at it until it disappeared from view. When Russell looked back to the zip line path, he saw the ground approaching.

Once he landed, Russell looked around. The zip line left them farther inland. He had to search for the sign that pointed toward the river.

Waiting for the others, he thought about the green team and how big their lead would be by now. It wasn't long before his teammates were all on the ground, taking off their harnesses.

"The new clue came in," Dev announced, holding up the ancam.


```
Deep pink in dark water,
    Gray in the clear.
No need to see your dinner,
    If you can always hear.
```

"Well, that's another winner," Dev said.

"I don't know what it is, but it says something about the water, so I think we should go back to the river," Sage announced. "We'll figure it out on the boat." She headed toward the path to the dock. Dev glanced at Russell and Mari, then followed Sage.

"Wait," Mari said, almost in a whisper.

Russell was the only one who heard her.

"I've almost got it," she said. She pressed her fingertips into either side of her head.

"Wait, you guys!" Russell called. When he looked up, he realized Dev and Sage had already turned down the lush, forest path. He could barely see them. "You guys, wait a sec!" He glanced back at Mari, who was still deep in thought.

Just as Sage and Dev came back around the turn, Russell heard a low rumbling sound.

"What?" Sage yelled. She didn't look happy.

Russell didn't answer. He was trying to make out the sound. Then he heard it again. It was a growl, and now it was getting closer.

"Uh-oh," announced Sage. She stopped short.

Between them was a jaguar cub. Blue-eyed, spotted, and fluffy, the cub was too young to be on its own.

The growl grew deeper.

"That's not coming from this little guy. It's the cub's mom," Sage called from down the path. "We need to get out of here. You've got to run the other way. Fast!"

CREATURE FEATURE

PALE-THROATED
THREE-TOED SLOTH

SCIENTIFIC NAME: *Bradypus tridactylus*

TYPE: mammal

RANGE: rain forests of Central and South America

FOOD: tree leaves, twigs, and buds

What is the size of a house cat, lives upside down, and is one of the slowest animals in the world? The sloth! The three-toed sloth has long, curved claws. Its claws are strong enough that the sloth can hang from them all day, even while it sleeps, which is a lot. The length of its claws makes it hard for the sloth to move on the ground, so these animals are safest high in the canopy. Sloths often have a green tint to their long hair; it's because algae, a kind of plant, lives there.

There are other three-toed sloths and also two-toed sloths, but they are all different species.

CHAPTER 6

A GOOD PREDATOR

Russell saw the movement in the leaves. He grabbed Mari's hand and took off, trying to get as far from the jaguar cub as possible. He knew that the cub would be the mother's first concern.

"Meet at the boat!" Sage's voice seemed to fade as she and Dev ran down the path. Russell and Mari forged deeper into the forest.

They ran until they had to stop, Russell's shallow breath burning in the back of his throat.

"I can't believe we saw a jaguar. They're incredibly endangered and very private animals." While Mari was marveling about their good fortune, Russell was thinking that their fortune was not so good at all. Looking around, he realized how foolish they had been. They had run without thinking, without noting landmarks.

"I still hear something," Russell said. The rain forest was always full of sound, but this was the sound of a large group of animals: leaves rustling, twigs breaking. "Come on," he said, grabbing Mari's hand again. He jogged, skirting fallen branches. He stopped. "I still hear it."

That's when he saw the tree. Its top branches opened like a giant green umbrella in the sky, nearly two hundred feet high. But Russell was interested in the tree's base. He pulled Mari toward it. Many leg-like roots sprouted from the trunk, making the tree look like a sea monster rising from the wet earth. Russell didn't care. He had seen a gap between the gnarled roots. Ducking down, he tried not to think of the hundreds of species that would call a dark hollow like this home. He pulled off his backpack and slid through the opening.

It was dark, and the damp air smelled rich.

"A good predator could sniff us out in here," Mari insisted.

Russell brought his finger to his lips. "A good predator wouldn't break twigs," he whispered, "telling us it was close."

He knew Mari understood. He had thought it was the jaguar following them at first, too, but jaguars were too clever to be detected. Russell knelt down, hidden by the shadows, and listened. Beyond the soft scurrying and odd, dripping sounds under the tree, he could hear something else. There were voices, coming closer.

"Where'd they go?"

Russell recognized that voice at once. It was Gabe.

"I don't know. It says they should be here," Dallas replied.

Even in the darkness, Russell could see Mari's eyes grow wide as she realized it was the green team.

"Maybe it's broken. Maybe Russell's team didn't come this way at all."

Russell tried to peek out, but he couldn't see anything. What was Dallas looking at?

"It was working before."

"It doesn't matter. Russell doesn't know where he's going. Or maybe he lost his backpack. We have to get back to the river. Maybe our guide can give us a hint."

That was Jayden. No one responded to him. They just took off, heading back the way they came.

"What was that all about?" Mari asked as she and Russell squeezed their way out in the open.

"I can't say," Russell answered. "You heard the same thing. It sounded like they followed us."

"But why?" Mari wondered.

Russell shook his head as he brushed ants off his legs. Even though he had a sneaking suspicion as to how his friends had found them, he really couldn't say, not unless he wanted to get them kicked out of the race for good. For now, he decided to focus on his own team.

"We've gotta move," Russell insisted, but Mari was facing in the opposite direction. She shifted her backpack and buckled it at her chest before she turned around.

"We came from that way, didn't we?" Mari asked, pointing. There was doubt in her voice.

"I don't think so," Russell said, noticing tracks on the ground. "It looks like the green team went this way."

Without another word, they set off at a jog. Russell quickly lost the green team's path. Mari was not fast, but she was steady. It gave Russell time to try to pick the best route. It was hard to tell if they were headed in the right direction. He led Mari downhill, hoping the slope would lead to the river, only to find that the land pitched uphill again.

"Wait," Mari said after a while, coming to a full stop. "Nothing looks familiar." She had turned back and was facing the opposite direction again. To Russell, this part of the forest looked pretty much like all the others: moss everywhere, endless trees, emerald leaves overhead, dead leaves on the ground.

Russell would never admit it, but he was certain they were lost.

ENDANGERED SPECIES AND HABITAT

Many species in the Amazon rain forest are endangered. *Endangered* is a term for an animal that could become extinct in the near future. An animal becomes extinct when there are no longer any of its kind alive. These are some of the Amazonian animals that are endangered:

black spider monkey

golden lion tamarin monkey

great green macaw

Amazonian glass frog

Many other animals, including both predators and prey, are on the verge of being endangered. They are considered "near threatened" or "vulnerable." Some of these include:

harpy eagle

jaguar

maned wolf

lowland tapir

The greatest threat to these animals is the loss of habitat. Since the 1960s, the lush forest has been replaced by farms, ranches, and roads. The loss of rain forest habitat is a tremendous threat to animals, plants, and humans alike.

CHAPTER 7

PRETTY iN PiNK

Mari flinched, her whole body tense. Russell watched as she raised her chin and stared up toward the sky, alert like a cat. "Hear that sound?" she whispered.

Russell could hear lots of sounds, all running together. He listened closer. He didn't hear anything like when the green team had been tracking them.

"It's the squirrel cuckoo," Mari said. "The same call again and again." She flashed an unexpected smile at Russell and moved toward the sound. She tilted her head to the side, as if her ear were leading the way. "I bet that's not a real bird," she mumbled. "I haven't seen any squirrel cuckoos around. It's Sage and Dev, using the bird calls, taking turns."

Russell followed Mari, stunned that she could tease the laughing squawk of the squirrel cuckoo out of the constant chorus of the forest.

Before long, they stepped into a small clearing. Russell recognized it at once.

"I saw this," he said, almost in a daze. "From the zip line."

At the clearing's center was a stone monument. Covered in ancient carvings, it was evidence of the old civilizations of the Amazon. Russell stopped and stared. He knew that people lived in the rain forest, but they had not seen any signs of them. Looking at the monument, Russell realized that it was in the shape of a tree—the same kind of tree where he and Mari had hidden from the green team.

"Russell, come on," Mari said from the far side of the clearing. "If you saw this from the zip line, then we're really close. And, you might recall," she added, in a tone not unlike Sage's, "this is a race."

When they finally found their way to the river, the smiles of Javier, Sage, and Dev lifted their spirits. Their teammates were thrilled to learn that the green team was not that far ahead.

"That's awesome," Sage said as they all took seats in the boat. "They haven't come back to the dock yet, so we might even be in the lead. We just have to answer the clue."

Dev unclipped the ancam from his utility belt and read it again. "I figure the last two lines, about not seeing your dinner if you can hear, could be about echolocation," Dev said. "You know, using sonar. Lots of animals can make a sound, and then visualize things based on the sound waves that echo back to them."

"Yeah, like bats," said Sage.

"And dolphins," Russell added.

"That's it!" Mari yelled. "The Amazon river dolphin. I couldn't come up with it before. It uses echolocation. And, in really murky water, the dolphin is pink. But it's gray when the water's clear. It has to do with their skin getting more sun or something."

"Awesome. So we just have to find a river dolphin now. I assume in the river?" Sage said.

The question was directed at Mari, but everyone smirked.

"Yes," Mari answered, still trying not to laugh. "During the rainy season, they venture into the streams and the flooded areas, but they'd be in the river now."

"So, do you all agree to go downriver?" Javier asked. They agreed.

"All right, sir. Let's go," Javier said, pointing.

The captain nodded. "Anchors aweigh," he said with a smile, even though the motorboat didn't have an anchor.

After a few moments, Sage whispered, "Should we ask if we can go faster?"

"Well, we probably have a better chance of seeing a dolphin if we aren't going too fast," Mari said. "Even then, it'll take some luck."

The team went silent.

"Fish?" the captain said.

"No." Sage shook her head. "We need a dolphin."

"No, fish," he repeated.

Russell looked toward the captain and noticed that he was pointing to a bucket of fish. "You have fish!" Russell yelled out. "We can use them to lure a dolphin," Russell said. "Thank you!" He grabbed the bucket with both hands. The captain smiled, his eyes bright like the sun on water.

Javier spoke with the captain and confirmed that it was a good location for tracking down dolphins. "He said there is a dock close by where tourists even swim with them."

It took only a few minutes of throwing in fish and peering into the cloudy water before a pale pink beak poked out. The dolphin turned to look at the boat. "Quick, Dev!" Russell said.

Sage threw a fish in the air, and the dolphin snapped its long, skinny jaw shut.

"Got it!" Dev cried.

"They have a brain capacity forty percent larger than humans," Mari said, almost absentmindedly.

Russell looked at the dolphin again—its pink head freckled with gray, its tiny round eyes and open grin. He thought how amazing it would be to swim with them. For a moment, he wished it wasn't a race.

"I've got the next clue," Dev said.


```
   Pass where the waters meet,
Then you'll find flags that greet.
```

Follow the path marked for you,
And LEARN the Amazon's final clue.

"That's horrible," Dev said. "My little brother can rhyme better than that."

"I believe you," Sage responded. "But let's make a decision. Do we keep going downstream?" The team nodded.

"Hang on," the captain said, shifting the tiller. The motor strained and the boat pitched forward.

It wasn't long before the sound of the motor was drowned out.

Russell turned to see a larger boat approaching, its nose lifted high. The boat revved by, the noisy motor churning up waves. Russell gripped the side of their smaller boat as it lurched in the rough water. The word that came to his mind was *rude*.

"No way!" Russell heard Dev cry, his voice carrying over the *thrum* of the engines.

"How'd *they* get *that* boat?" Sage asked.

Russell didn't want to look. When he did, he saw what he already knew: It was the green team.

"I don't know," Javier answered, shaking his head. "Maybe that boat showed up after we left. It definitely wasn't one of the ones at the dock."

Russell watched as the other boat disappeared around one of the Amazon's many turns. It was clear that the red team's tiny boat was already going at top speed. The only thing to do was watch and wait.

Except Russell did have something to do. Trying not to be obvious, he examined his backpack. He had wanted to do it ever since the green team showed up at the giant tree.

He soon found what he was looking for. It looked like a merit badge—a fabric patch with a four-leaf clover on it. It was stuck there with some kind of glue. It blended into the backpack's original design.

When he ripped off the patch, he found a tiny chip underneath. Now he had proof. His friends had been tracking him. Dallas had probably snagged some kind of GPS device from his mom's office. No wonder the green team had gone upstream to find the capybara. Russell's gut knotted when he realized that they were still tracking him. They must have noticed that the red team's boat had stopped in the river, just long enough to snap a photo of a friendly Amazon river dolphin. Russell would bet anything that the green team had followed them to that point, stopped their big motorboat, and photographed the same one.

At first, Russell was going to just drop the chip in the river. He wanted to be rid of it. Then he thought again. It wasn't safe to drop an electronic device in the water. What if a fish ate it? So he pocketed the chip. He'd decide what to do later.

He glanced over at Javier, whose expression

was as serious as his teammates'. Javier seemed to realize Russell was watching him. "I don't know how they got that faster boat," he said.

Russell shrugged. "It's always something," he offered. Russell had heard his dad say that tons of times when another team had made a good play. It was Dad's way of reminding him that nothing's ever easy, but you have to keep trying. Russell had to remind himself of that now.

"Hey, Javier," Russell said, trying to think of something else. "I saw some kind of stone monument from the zip line. It was all carved. It looked like people made it a long time ago."

"Yes, I know it," Javier said. "It is a symbol for the kapok, or the world tree. The people of this region believe the tree is sacred. It reaches up to the heavens with its limbs, and down into the earth with its roots. The kapok tree represents how all life is connected."

Russell nodded, his hand still resting on the chip in his pocket. He liked that idea.

"What is that?" Dev yelled, loud enough for everyone to hear.

Russell looked toward the middle of the river, where Dev was staring.

Dev put his hand on Mari's shoulder for balance and stood up. "That water is a totally different color," he said.

"Dev, that's it! I know why the river changes color like that," Sage exclaimed. "This is where the waters meet!"

LIFE IN THE FOREST

Today, hundreds of thousands of people live in the Amazon rain forest. There are over 400 tribes, and the people speak at least 180 different languages. Some of these people follow traditional customs that are hundreds of years old. They make their own tools, hunt and gather in the forest, and carve canoes from the giant kapok tree. But the influence of the outside world has changed life in many villages.

Archaeologists have found evidence that there were once many well-organized civilizations in the Amazon that were far larger than those of today. There were up to seven million people making their life in the rain forest around 500 hundred years ago. However, when explorers arrived from overseas in the 1500s, they brought diseases with them. Many of these diseases, like smallpox, were foreign to the Amazonian people, and great numbers of them died.

The people who live in the rain forest today are still resourceful. They know which plants to eat, which to use as medicine, and which to avoid because they are poisonous . . . or not tasty. For hundreds of years, they have sustained their lives and the livelihood of the forest.

CHAPTER 8

A FRAYED FRIENDSHIP

"**T**his has to be it!" Sage yelled again. "The river we are on now is the Amazon, and that must be the River Negro," she explained. "See how that river is darker than the Amazon? For a while, the waters don't mix. They flow separately, side by side."

Russell's eyebrows tightened. How did Sage know something like that? Mari must have wondered the same thing, because she asked.

"It's all my sister," Sage confessed. "She did a

whole science fair project on erosion in American rivers. Don't ask. She's a whiz."

"Whenever it rains, which is a lot, the rainwater carries soil and nutrients into the water," Javier said. "That's where the color comes from. It's the same with the Amazon River, but it's greener."

As if on cue, it started to drizzle. It had been so muggy, the rain felt good.

"So?" Dev said, looking at their guide. "Is this it?"

"I can't tell you. Maybe you should reread the clue."

Dev did just that, cringing again at the bad rhymes. Then everyone started looking for the "flags that greet." Sage and Dev searched on one side. Mari and Russell searched the other.

Russell soon noticed several pennant-shaped flags with the Wild Life logo. The flags marked a path, leading up from the muddy beach. The larger, faster motorboat was already there.

"At least there's only one boat," Dev pointed out. "We're probably in second place." They hadn't seen any of the other teams since the start of the race, so they hadn't had any idea what place they were in.

"It's not over yet," Sage said, splashing her rubber boot into the river before the boat had reached the shore. Russell sprang out next, landing in the muck. Dev and Mari followed.

"Good luck!" Javier called out.

The four kids turned and waved before charging up the stone-lined path. When they reached the crest of the hill, they found that the ground dropped again immediately. A deep gulley cut through the land, with a ribbon of water the color of chocolate milk at the very bottom.

"How are we supposed to cross this?" Mari wondered out loud.

"There's another pennant over there." Dev pointed downstream, and the group jogged along the narrow ridge, forcing their way through the lush growth.

Sage crouched down as soon as she reached the point across from the flag. "No way," she hissed.

The rest of the team gathered around. Russell couldn't believe it either.

"The green team cut the rope bridge, so no one else could cross?" Dev said as he looked at the far side of the gulley. "That hardly seems sportsmanlike."

Russell could see the frayed stubs of thick, grayed rope, dangling down the far side of the ditch.

"That's the only explanation I can think of," Sage answered, lifting up the other end of the bridge. The wooden slats clacked against the dirt wall when she let go.

Russell still didn't believe it. Would his friends seriously pull something like that? This was all his fault. If he hadn't been foolish enough to let them track him, they'd never have been in the lead in the first place. Now it was up to him to find another way to get his team across. "It's steep, but we could slide down, wade through the water, and climb up the other side," he suggested.

"That is not an option," Mari said, with uncommon certainty. "There are piranhas down there.

I know they aren't usually that dangerous to humans, but that's a shallow streambed where there are not a lot of food options. That's a desperate scenario for piranhas—and us."

Russell gulped, then glanced around. His gaze traveled up the trees and across to the other side. "The vines," he said. "We can swing across."

"Seriously?" Sage said. "You've seen too many adventure movies."

"You got a better idea?" Russell had already looked up and down the gulley. It didn't seem to have a beginning or end. "We don't want to get off the path with the flags. Come on," he said, tugging on one of the thick vines that twisted itself around a high branch.

"Not that one," Dev insisted, his gaze assessing the vine, the ditch, and the far bank. "It's set too far back. With that angle, it'll drop us in the middle of the stream. We need one closer to the edge." He took several paces, his eyes focused high in the branches. "One like this." Dev flung the vine across the expanse. The vine's tail dragged briefly on the other side.

Russell, Sage, and Mari stared as the vine traveled back.

"It's the best we'll get," Dev said, his voice confident. "I'll go first."

Russell held the lower part of the vine as Dev found his grip. "Ready?"

Mari shielded her eyes.

"Set," Dev said, and Russell grabbed Dev at the hips.

Russell took a step back and then ran forward and gave a firm shove. When he let go, Russell

swore part of him kept going across that open gulley, still on the vine with Dev.

As if he had timed it perfectly, Dev released at the exact moment the vine reached the height of its swing. He landed in a heap, but he didn't look hurt.

"Eeeeeeehhhhh!" squealed Sage. "Dev, are you okay?" She was jumping up and down for joy.

"It's kind of fun," Dev declared, pushing himself off the ground.

Mari had just managed to open her eyes. "He made it?" she asked.

"He made it," Sage said. "And you're going next."

CREATURE FEATURE

PIRANHA

SCIENTIFIC NAME: multiple species, family Characidae

TYPE: fish

RANGE: South American streams and rivers

FOOD: mostly fish, snails, and insects, but also plants and seeds, or sometimes birds or mammals

There are many species of piranhas, but they all have one thing in common: their sharp, triangular teeth. With its powerful jaws, the piranha can chomp a mouthful of meat with ease. The fish usually hunt alone. Group attacks are more likely in the dry season when water levels and food options are low. Despite their reputation, deadly piranha attacks on humans are rare.

CHAPTER 9

RACE TO THE FINISH

Dev had to practically pull Mari off the vine, but she made it across in one piece. Sage was next, and Russell wasn't surprised when she landed on the other bank with a graceful release. Just as she whipped the vine back his way, he heard the puttering of a motor nearby. Then the motor stopped.

"It's another team!" he yelled. "They just docked. You guys have to move. I'll catch up."

He was surprised when they didn't need convincing. The rest of his team took off on a narrow path through ferns and palms.

The raindrops had increased to jungle size. Russell had never been this wet with his clothes on. He wiped his eyes and looked at the gulley ahead. Russell had given everyone else a push. Now he had to get himself across. He needed a running start. He stepped back, and then took off. His feet thudded against the ground, and his upper arms tensed as he pulled himself onto the vine, his blistered hands throbbing. There wasn't time to feel the wind in his hair. The vine was swinging back before he knew it. Russell let go and skidded down the far side of the gulley, dropping closer and closer to the piranha pool. His fingers grasped a loose root, then another, and he scrambled up to high ground. He lay on his back for a moment, savoring the taste of dirt in his mouth. He wasn't just wet now, he was caked in mud.

It took the calls of unfamiliar voices to remind him that he wasn't on the football field. No, he was on the first leg of *The Wild Life*, just steps from the day's final clue! He crawled to his knees, to his feet, picking up pace as he passed the first flag on the far side of the gulley. The piranhas hadn't gotten a piece of him, and he wasn't going to let the other racers either. He had to meet up with his team.

He could still taste the dirt as he ran up a steep flight of stone stairs. When he reached the top, he realized he was standing on an overhang that looked out on a waterfall. There was a wooden railing only feet from the gushing water. At first, Russell just wanted to marvel at the sight. But Bull Gordon stood right in front of the waterfall. Off to his right was the green team. The other members of the red team were off to his left.

"Russell," Bull announced, "welcome. Now that the entire red team is here, I can announce that you are the second to arrive." Russell felt his teeth grit with a smile, but his teammates were serious. Bull continued, "The green team was first, but they have failed to answer the final clue. I will now give it to you. We'll see if your team can answer it."

As soon as Bull Gordon handed Russell the envelope, his three teammates huddled close. With trembling fingers, he ripped it open. "Hurry,

hurry, hurry," Sage chanted nervously. At the top of the card was the same logo that had been on the flags. Directly below was the clue.

```
Straight toward the heavens,
    An umbrella of green,
Almost an entire ecosystem
     Alive in one tree.
```

Russell blinked and thought about the last two lines. An ecosystem meant that it was a community of living things that all work together. A healthy ecosystem is balanced.

Mari looked at him, hopeful. "You know it, don't you?"

"Yeah," Russell said. "I think I do." He told his teammates what he remembered. He remembered the tree they saw in the leafy canopy with the bromeliad that was a frog nursery. It grew hundreds of feet tall and held eagle nests in its top branches. It was also the kind of tree where he and Mari had hid, among the thousands of insects, when the green team had followed them.

The four kids approached Bull Gordon together.

Russell looked at each teammate in turn. They all nodded. "Is it the kapok tree?" he asked, his voice lifting on the last word.

Bull Gordon raised his scarred chin. "Indeed it is," he said. "Team Red, you are the first to complete this leg of the race. You will have a head start on the next leg."

Russell felt chills start in his shoulders and branch out in every direction. The red team didn't yelp or cheer, but they all exchanged hugs. They had done it.

"That's not fair," Jayden said, loud enough for everyone to hear. "The answer was a kind of tree, not an animal. This is supposed to be about wildlife."

The red team paused their small celebration. Everyone looked to the host.

"I tend to think an animal's habitat is very important," Bull Gordon said to the entire group, his thumbs punching through his belt loops. "The kapok tree provides food and homes to countless rain forest creatures. It is the perfect example of how all the organisms in an ecosystem are connected and rely on one another."

Russell let out a sigh and noticed Sage studying him.

"I figured it out," she said.

"What?" Russell asked.

"What I asked you earlier, what you have to offer."

Russell thought back to the day before. It seemed so long ago.

"You know what it means to be on a team," Sage said. "And that's all we could ask for. Thanks."

"Thanks to you, too," Russell replied, laughing it off. But he meant it. It mattered.

One by one, the members of the green team came up to congratulate him. "At least one of us came in first," Damien said with a friendly high five. "We're all in this together after all, man." Russell gave an uncertain nod.

When Dallas approached, he wore his typical post-game grin. He patted Russell on the shoulder. "Glad your team is solid," he said. "Maybe we can work together on the next leg."

"Maybe," replied Russell, but he didn't look his old friend in the eye. Dallas had cheated, and Russell didn't know what to do about it. It wasn't right. They shouldn't get away with it, but Russell didn't want the green team to be kicked out of the race either. He'd been friends with them for a long time, and he didn't want the race to change that.

Instead, his gaze turned to Mari, Dev, and Sage—his new team. His new friends. He hoped that if they ever found out what he knew, they wouldn't be too disappointed in him.

He could hear the yells of another group approaching. Who knew, maybe that team would be their real competition on the next leg. Together, the red team had survived and succeeded in the rain forest, and Russell was already looking forward to what would come next.

Want to know what happens when *The Wild Life* moves to the Great Barrier Reef? Read on for a glimpse of the next race course in

Just then, a motorboat appeared from behind the nearby island. Javier waved it down. "Get ready for your first challenge," he announced. He held out a canvas box and raised the lid. Inside was what looked like a smartphone, with a short antenna. "The ancam!" Dev declared, plunging his hand into the box.

"You sound so excited," Russell said in a mocking tone. Dev had hated the ancam at first, but had quickly mastered the tiny device that combined a walkie-talkie and camera. It was how they received directions and clues from the race organizers. It was also how they submitted their answers so they could move on to the next clue.

"It's time," said Javier. "Get yourselves over to that boat."

"You got it?" Sage asked Dev, making sure he

would take charge of their communications device. Dev held up the ancam and gave a confident grin.

Sage instinctively checked for both earrings, then dove in. The chill of the water made everything feel real. The race really was on now. With powerful stokes, she made her way to the other vessel.

After she climbed the ladder to the small deck, she looked back at her teammates. Dev wasn't far behind. His thick black hair was even straighter than usual, wet against his dark skin. Russell, despite his athletic frame and busy schedule of team sports, did not appear to be a strong swimmer. His kick was sloppy, and his breathing lacked an even rhythm. But Mari was struggling even more. When she finally reached the ladder, Sage reached out and gave her a hand. Mari looked disoriented with the salt water streaming down her face. "You okay?" Sage asked.

"I think so," Mari answered, immediately sitting on the bench at the side of the deck.

Sage turned to the captain of the boat and her first mate. Both wore long-sleeved rash guards for sun protection. With the same sparkly blue eyes and space between their front teeth, they looked like mother and son.

"Hi," Sage said. "We're part of *The Wild Life.*"

"We know," answered the woman. "That's why we're here. I'm Gayle. This is Cole."

"We've got our next clue!" Dev announced, holding up the ancam. "I'll read it."

Two will start by flying high
To get a prime view from the sky.

Search and it will be no fluke
When your team sights a true fluke.

"Yuck. They need to get new writers," Dev declared. "You can't rhyme a word with the same word."

"But they have different meanings," Mari insisted.

"It doesn't matter. It's horrendous. And embarrassing."

"Who cares?" Sage called out, throwing up her arms. "We have a clue!" She turned back to Gayle. "Is this a parasail boat?" she asked, eyeing the gear near the boat's stern.

"Sure is. I need two volunteers."

"Dev, you should come with me," Sage said as she grabbed a pair of binoculars. When he paused, she added, "You're the one with the ancam."

Dev looked to Mari and Russell, then stepped into place next to Sage. There was a blur of buckles and snaps and straps as they put on life jackets and harnesses.

"Mari, any advice?" Sage asked.

"Well," Mari began, "there are fish called flukes, but I don't think any live around here, or are big enough to see from way up there." Mari squinted as she looked into the sky. "So you must be looking for a whale fluke—two flukes make up a whale's tail. You can see them when humpback whales breach. That's when they throw themselves out of the water. It's really beautiful."

Sage nodded. Maybe she should have chosen

Mari to parasail with her. But Dev was the techie. She knew he'd get the best shot.

"Now is a good time to see humpbacks," Mari continued. "They've just migrated. Even in winter, the Great Barrier Reef is warmer than the Arctic."

With breakneck speed, Gayle and Cole latched Sage into place on the small gondola. It reminded Sage of a ski lift. Dev paused, several steps away. His eyes seemed to be darting around, focusing on one thing and then another. At last, he came forward so Gayle and Cole could strap him in, too.

With the pull of a lever, Gayle released the parachute, which billowed behind the boat. The sail lifted and took Sage and Dev with it. Sage felt her stomach lurch.

"What were you looking at back there?" she asked.

"I was trying to figure out if this thing was safe," Dev yelled over the swirling wind. "My dad would freak out if he could see me."

"Why?"

"He's an engineer. He is very concerned with the way things work."

Sage had been so set on the race that she hadn't even paused to think about safety. With all that had happened in the last year, she was surprised she hadn't considered it. But her focus was always on the finish line. "Remember, we're looking for whales," she said, concentrating on things she could control. "Breaching whales, so that we can see a fluke."

Sage took in the full view. They were now

hundreds of feet in the air. Below them, the water was deep blue. Toward the mainland, she could see the reef. The water there was shallow and appeared much brighter. She could see how it was many reefs, hugging the coast. They looked like turquoise jewels from up high, strung together like an expensive necklace. It was hard to believe that something so big was alive—and that the animals that made the reef were tiny.

"It's amazing up here," Sage yelled. The wind plastered loose strands of hair across her face.

"Yeah," Dev agreed. "I wish Russell and Mari could see it."

"Yeah," she said.

"Check it out!" Dev demanded, pointing at the ancam. "They added a telephoto lens! They kind of had to. We could never get a decent shot without it." Mari had told them that she had read in the folder about how there was a buffer zone for whale watching. No boat could get within a hundred yards of a whale for safety reasons.

Dev lifted the handheld device to his eye and tried to focus in on something below. "Hey, look," he said excitedly.

"What?" Sage asked hopefully.

"Russell's driving the boat."

"I thought you were worried about safety," Sage said.

"They won't let him do anything drastic," Dev answered, but just as he said it, the gondola took a dip.

"Whoa!" Sage yelled. It felt like all her organs had jumped into her throat. "What was that?"

Dev scanned the water's surface. "They must have spotted something . . ."

READ *GREAT REEF GAMES* TO FIND OUT WHAT HAPPENS NEXT!